Maths Together

There's a lot more to maths than numbers and sums; it's an important language which helps us describe, explore and explain the world we live in. So the earlier children develop an appreciation and understanding of maths, the better.

We use maths all the time – when we shop or travel from one place to another, for example. Even when we fill the kettle we are estimating and judging quantities. Many games and puzzles involve maths. So too do stories and poems, often in an imaginative and interesting way.

Maths Together is a collection of high-quality picture books designed to introduce children, simply and enjoyably, to basic mathematical ideas – from counting and measuring to pattern and probability. By listening to the stories and rhymes, talking about them and asking questions, children will gain the confidence to try out the mathematical ideas for themselves – an important step in their numeracy development.

You don't have to be a mathematician to help your child learn maths. Just as by reading aloud you play a vital role in their literacy development, so by sharing the *Maths Together* books with your child, you will play an important part in developing their understanding of mathematics. To help you, each book has detailed notes at the back, explaining the mathematical ideas that it introduces, with suggestions for further related activities.

With *Maths Together*, you can count on doing the very best for your child.

To Richard and Mongolia
with love J.B.

N.S.

First published 1999 by Walker Books Ltd
87 Vauxhall Walk, London SE11 5HJ

2 4 6 8 10 9 7 5 3 1

Text © 1999 Jeannie Billington
Illustrations © 1999 Nicola Smee
Introductory and concluding notes
© 1999 Jeannie Billington and Grace Cook

This book has been typeset in Calligraphic 810 BT.

Printed in Singapore

British Library Cataloguing in Publication Data
A catalogue record for this book is
available from the British Library.

ISBN 0-7445-6837-4 (hb)
ISBN 0-7445-6800-5 (pb)

SIX FEET LONG
AND
THREE FEET WIDE

Jeannie Billington

Illustrated by
Nicola Smee

WALKER BOOKS
AND SUBSIDIARIES
LONDON • BOSTON • SYDNEY

Erdine was tall for her age. When she was nine she was nearly as tall as her father. When she was ten her feet dangled right off the end of her little wooden bed.

Erdine's father had an idea.
"I'll ask Nasan the carpenter to make Erdine a new bed for her eleventh birthday," he said. "He can have one of my fine horses as payment."

Erdine lay down on the floor so Nasan could measure her.

"One ... two ... three ... four ... five ... SIX FEET LONG!" said Nasan. "My, she is tall for her age!"

Nasan went home to begin work on the bed for Erdine. But it was a warm afternoon and he felt rather sleepy.

"Damdiny," he said to his youngest son, "you start work on the bed while I have a little rest. And be sure to make it six feet long and three feet wide. Chop-chop!"

Damdiny started work straight away.
He counted carefully.

"One ... two ... three ... four ... five ... six feet long," and

"one ... two ... three feet wide."
He sawed and hammered and planed and carved, until long after the sun had set.
At last his work was finished. Damdiny lay down on the bed he had made and fell asleep.

The next morning Nasan and Damdiny carried the bed to Erdine's house.

"It's beautiful!" said Erdine, and she lay down on it.
But, oh dear. The bed was much too small.

"Damdiny," snapped Nasan, "measure the bed."
Damdiny measured the bed with his feet:
"One ... two ... three ... four ... five ... six feet
long," and "one ... two ... three feet wide."

"There you are!" said Nasan to Erdine's father.
"Just as you ordered. Now where's my payment?"

"Father," said Damdiny in a small voice.
He placed his foot next to Nasan's.
"You measured Erdine with your feet, and
your feet are almost twice as big as mine."

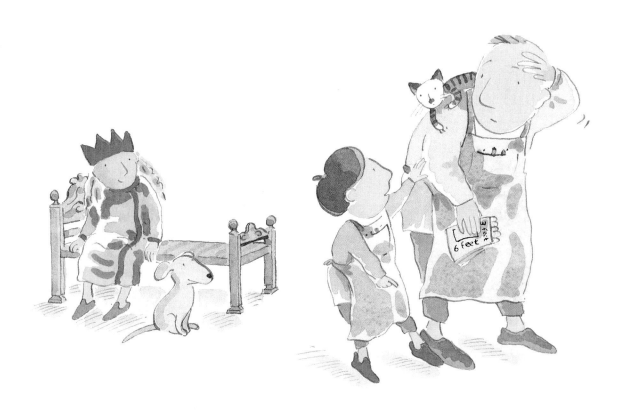

Nasan was speechless. "I ... I..."
His face turned beetroot red. "I ... we ...
you see..."
Then he turned to Damdiny and bellowed:
"Well, naturally when I said six feet I meant
six of *my* feet, not yours. Foolish boy!"

Back in his workshop, Nasan measured out the wood for another bed for Erdine with his own large feet. Then he ordered Damdiny to finish the job.

Damdiny worked all night, and in the morning he and Nasan carried the new bed to Erdine's house.

"It's beautiful!" cried Erdine, and she
lay down on it. "And it's just the right size!"
"Happy birthday, Erdine," said Erdine's
father, and he kissed her.

"Now," said Nasan. "My payment ... the horse
you promised me?"
"I'll choose one of my finest horses and have
it brought to you today," smiled Erdine's father.
"Be sure to choose a chestnut mare, ten hands
high," said Nasan.
And he and Damdiny went off home.

Erdine went straight to the stables to choose the horse herself. She found Millie, her favourite chestnut mare, and measured her carefully with her hands.
"One ... two ... three ... four ... five ... six ... seven ... eight ... nine ... TEN HANDS HIGH. Perfect!" said Erdine.

Erdine took Millie to the house of Nasan
the carpenter. Nasan was delighted.
He saddled her up and mounted her...

But, oh dear. The horse was much too small.

"Foolish girl," fumed Nasan. "I said ten hands high ... ten of *my* hands, not yours!"
Erdine smiled. "But Nasan," she said, "this horse is just right for Damdiny."

And, do you know, she was right!

About this book

Six Feet Long and Three Feet Wide is about length.

To make the right-sized bed for Erdine, Nasan the carpenter needs to measure both Erdine and the bits of wood in his workshop. He uses his feet to measure Erdine, then his son Damdiny measures the wood with *his* feet. It's Damdiny who first realizes the problem: to compare the two lengths properly, they need to use the same unit of measurement.
The story is a good way of introducing this difficult concept to children. Measuring with you at home will give them the chance to learn it first-hand.

There are other lessons about measurement to be learned from the book, too. Because Nasan is bigger, it takes fewer of his feet than Damdiny's to measure the wood. Noticing this helps children understand the idea that the larger the unit of measurement, the fewer the units needed to measure.

Also, while it's important that Erdine's bed is big enough, it doesn't have to be an exact fit. When measuring how long something is you don't always have to be exact – sometimes a bit of string, hands or feet are good enough. At other times, when accuracy is needed, standard measurements like metres and millimetres are used.

You can talk about these ideas and how they apply to other measurements too: weight, volume, capacity, area and time.

Notes for parents

As you re-read the story, pause when Erdine finds out the bed's too small for her, and again when Nasan finds out the horse is too small for him. Ask your child if they know *why* they're too small.

Children compare things and put them in order all the time. It helps them to understand how wide, how deep, how high and how far things are.

Sometimes your child will want to measure something more accurately. Talk together about how you might do this.

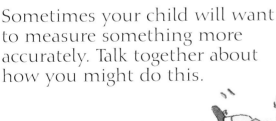

You and your child can use old magazines to make footprints or handprints for measuring. Draw round your feet and hands and cut out lots of prints, then go on a "measuring trail" and compare your results.

Once they've got the feel of measuring, you can stop your child halfway through measuring something and ask them to estimate how many hands or feet it will be altogether. See if they can explain their answer and then check it.

It's important to be encouraging. With practice, children's estimates become more accurate – what matters at this stage is having a go.

Children learn a lot from seeing you measure things, and hearing you talk about what you are doing.

A height chart is a great way to measure children's growth and that of family and friends. You can buy one or make your own on a long strip of paper stuck to the wall.
On each birthday, record your child's height and the date.

Maths Together

The *Maths Together* programme is divided into two sets – yellow (age 3+) and green (age 5+). There are six books in each set, helping children learn maths through story, rhyme, games and puzzles.

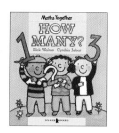
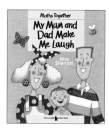

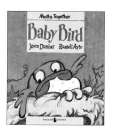

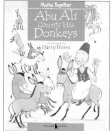